Room
555

Room 555

Cristy Watson

ORCA BOOK PUBLISHERS

Library and Archives Canada Cataloguing in Publication

Watson, Cristy, 1964–, author
Room 555 / Cristy Watson.
(Orca currents)

Issued in print and electronic formats.
ISBN 978-1-4598-2058-6 (softcover).—ISBN 978-1-4598-2059-3 (pdf).—
ISBN 978-1-4598-2060-9 (epub)

I. Title. II. Title: Room five hundred fifty-five.
III. Series: Orca currents
PS8645.A8625R66 2019   jc813'.6   c2018-904871-9
c2018-904872-7

First published in the United States, 2019
Library of Congress Control Number: 2018952761

Summary: In this high-interest novel for middle readers,
Roonie struggles to deal with her grandmother's declining health.

*Orca Book Publishers is dedicated to preserving the environment and
has printed this book on Forest Stewardship Council® certified paper.*

Orca Book Publishers gratefully acknowledges the support for its
publishing programs provided by the following agencies: the Government
of Canada, the Canada Council for the Arts and the Province of British
Columbia through the BC Arts Council and the Book Publishing Tax Credit.

Edited by Tanya Trafford
Cover artwork by iStock.com/FatCamera
Author photo by Lynne Woodley

ORCA BOOK PUBLISHERS
orcabook.com

Printed and bound in Canada.

22 21 20 19 • 4 3 2 1

For the real Jasmine, who inspires me every day. Thank you for your friendship. And for the young people I work with, who are brave enough to share their fears and worries as they navigate the world.

Chapter One

"Roonie, are you ready yet?" I can hear Jordan breathing outside my bedroom door. He is wheezing, and he only walked up the stairs. That boy needs to exercise!

"I'm not going!" I yell through the door. "Tell Mom I have too much homework."

"Like *you* do homework?"

"Just tell her I'm not going."

"Tell her yourself."

I tiptoe to the door and crack it open slightly. Even though my younger brother gets on my nerves, he usually follows through. He is a pro at sucking up to my parents. I hear him tell Dad I am staying home. He leaves off the homework part.

My dad is probably wearing his blue shirt and pink tie. He knows Gram loves it when he dresses up. Or at least she used to love seeing him in fancy clothes. Now I'm not sure what she sees—or remembers. She has been living at the Cedars Care Home for Seniors since I was ten. Three years she's been stuck in that place. I would die!

The stairs creak, and I know someone is coming up. As I close the door, I catch a whiff of my mom's perfume—lavender and rose. She smells nice, and I can tell she's doused herself with extra. Sometimes it smells bad in that place where they keep my grandma. Who am I kidding? It *always* smells bad in that place.

That is why I am not going. It smells like old, stale, forgotten people. And it is full of stale, old, forgotten people. We only have two days off from school, and I need to spend them practicing my hip-hop moves for the dance challenge. I am in my first year at high school, and they have a competition where I can even compete against twelfth graders. I would love to win.

But to do that, I have to practice. So it's not really like I am bailing on Gram. It's important that I do this competition. Then I will go visit her. Then I will have something to show her—a big trophy.

Since I closed my door when I first heard the creaky stairs, I don't know where Mom went. Maybe she had to grab something from her room, like her purse. She is always forgetting things or losing her stuff. But then I hear her heels clicking on the hardwood floor. She is standing outside my door.

"Roonie, may I come in?"

Before I can say no, she is turning my door handle. I fly across the room and land on my bed. It creaks too. It is probably as old as Gram.

"Do you mind, Mom? I could have been getting dressed. That's why I asked Dad to put a lock on the door."

"I'm sorry, Mary, but we need to talk."

I hate it when Mom uses my real name.

"It's too plain," I remember Gram saying one time when I was little. She was making my favorite spaghetti and meatballs. "You are meant for great things. Mary isn't a name that will make you soar." She had paused while she looked me over. "Macaroon! Now there's a name." It made us all laugh because Gram loves macaroons and made them for dessert every time we came to dinner.

Well, the name stuck and then got shortened to Roonie. I prefer that to Mary. Plus, Macaroon is a better name for a hip-hop dancer anyway.

Mom plops down on the bed beside me. That is lecture mode, and I am not interested. I jump up and cross my room to my desk. I pull open a binder and sit down on my blue exercise ball. Immediately my stomach muscles engage to keep me balanced on the ball.

"Look, Mom, I have tons of homework." That part is true. "I need to work on this for school on Monday or I may not pass the class." That part is true too. "I am going to work on it all afternoon." That part is not true. I plan to spend the afternoon on my hip-hop

5

routine for the dance contest. But Mom does not need to know that!

"It's just that you haven't been to visit Gram in months. She asks about you all the time. You used to love going. I know it's harder now because sometimes she doesn't remember us. But she loves you, and I know she misses you."

I get a lump in my throat. I love Gram too. But that place gives me the creeps. And I get way too emotional if Gram is having a bad day. I just want to remember her the way she was—painting, smiling and making macaroons.

"We are leaving in twenty minutes. We won't stay for long. Maybe you could work on your project when we get back?"

I shake my head. I feel guilty about not going with the family to see my grandmother. But it is so hard to see her like that. She used to be so beautiful, with her long dark hair. I can see her slender fingers holding the paintbrush as she made deep strokes along the canvas. Gram mostly did portraits. I tried painting with her one day, but I am definitely not an artist. Well, not *that* kind of artist. I am a hip-hop artist.

Mom sighs and leaves my room. I watch from my bedroom window as they pile into the car. As soon as it turns the corner, I grab my headphones. I push *Play*, and my favorite song blasts into my ears.

I have already changed into my sweatpants and tank top. I flex my arms in the mirror. Then, after shuffling my feet for a few moments to get my rhythm going, I bust a few moves. I do some side steps while criss-crossing my arms. Then I add some step-touches before I step-slide and drop to the floor. I love the stop-and-drop moves because then I can really get my groove on.

As I try a few pops and locks, Gram is no longer on my mind. I'm not thinking of her withering away in that place. I am not feeling guilty for bailing on her. I just feel the adrenaline flow through my body as I move to the music.

Chapter Two

At school on Tuesday, Ms. Burns, our school counselor, tells us we can begin our community volunteer hours. By twelfth grade we have to have some astronomical number of hours logged to get enough credits to graduate. I decide I should start now. Otherwise, I can see myself being Gram's age and still in high school!

I look over the list of places taking volunteers. At the bottom of the second page I see a dance studio. That would be perfect! Sure, it would mostly be answering phones and filing papers. But I would be around dancers. Maybe I'd get some ideas for my routine. I decide to sign up right after school. The forms are due back tomorrow.

On the way home my best friend, Kira, asks me if I want to do a routine with her for the dance competition. I usually prefer a solo act, but I have been watching *So You Think You Can Dance* and saw some cool routines for a duo. I figure why not? I stay at Kira's until suppertime, and we start planning our routine. After dinner I head home to work on my Social Studies project. I only take a few breaks to practice some new moves in front of the mirror.

The rest of the week is packed. On Wednesday I babysit for the McKenzies down the street. Their mom volunteers at Gram's care home sometimes and pays me twenty bucks for two hours of watching TV or playing video games with her two kids. Charlotte and Ben are pretty cool. Charlotte likes to dance. She is not into hip hop but takes tap-dancing lessons. She has taught me a few things that I was able to incorporate into my moves, like jumping up and landing on the toes of her taps. That move is a keeper!

On Thursday Mom picks us up from school. We're all getting haircuts. Jordan usually takes the longest at the salon. He likes his hair dyed blond on top, with dark roots underneath. I wish I could wear dreadlocks, but Mom won't hear of it.

The lady doing my hair smells like perm solution, and my nostrils burn. She talks about cutting my hair super short, says I have great bone structure.

Mom smiles and says, "Might be fun to try something different!" They don't get that my hair is part of my image.

"No, thanks. Just a trim."

Before I know it, it is Friday. The counselor comes into homeroom. Today is the day we get our volunteer placements. Oh no! I forgot to hand in the form!

"I will be passing around a sheet with the contact names for each of your placements. If you did not hand in your form, we chose a placement for you," says Ms. Burns.

Great. I'll probably get garbage pickup or something.

"You do not have to accept the placement we assigned to you, but there will not be another opportunity for volunteering again until next year," she continues.

If I leave it to next year, I will be super stressed about completing everything before graduation.

I bite my lip as the sheet comes to my desk. I look over at Kira. Her hair is streaked with pink today, matching her pink sneakers. She gives me a thumbs-up. I scan the sheet and stop at her name. OMG! She got the dance studio! Why didn't I get organized on time? Why did I leave it so late?

I scroll down and find my name. My contact person is Beth Adams. I am working at the hospital. "Oh no!" Everyone in homeroom turns to look at me. Oops, I meant to say that in my head. I shrug it off and laugh nervously. I look down at the sheet again. Sean, the guy sitting next to me, asks me to hurry up, because the bell will be going soon. He wants to know if he got his first pick.

First pick? I didn't know there would be several options. Now I am stuck with whatever they gave me. As I am scribbling down the contact information, I realize this might be okay. Maybe I will get a placement in the physio department. Somewhere like that would be okay. I could get ideas on how to limber up my body and take care of simple injuries. *Phew!*

My shoulders relax as I think about volunteering in a room full of exercise balls like the one I sit on at home. There might even be weights I could use and other equipment that will help strengthen my core.

As the bell goes, I look over to Kira and give her a thumbs-up.

Chapter Three

"Hi. I'm the new volunteer, and I'm here to see Ms. Adams." I am standing at the information desk at the hospital. The air smells like bleach. The receptionist points to the chairs behind me.

"Please take a seat. Ms. Adams will be with you shortly. You can fill out this form while you wait."

She hands me a clipboard with two pieces of paper attached to it and a pen dangling from a string. I grab a seat far away from the toddler sitting on her grandma's lap. Or maybe it is her great-grandma. The lady looks like she is ninety years old. The kid laughs every time her grandma wiggles her nose at her.

I look down at the sheet. I had hoped to volunteer somewhere cool, like the physio department. But I have been assigned to something called the geriatric wing. I don't even know what that means. I hope it has something to do with muscles or bones. Something that will fit with my passion for dance.

I finish filling in the form as quickly as I can. I am eager to find out what a geriatric room looks like and what I will be doing there. I am sure it will be great. When Ms. Adams walks into the waiting room and calls my name, I jump up to meet her. I hold out my hand, trying to be professional. This is my first time in the work force—even if it is just to volunteer.

"How are you doing today, Mary?"

"Roonie," I answer.

"I'm sorry?" says Ms. Adams as she reaches for the clipboard.

"Oh, I mean, I prefer to be called Roonie. And I'm fine, thanks." I feel heat rush into my cheeks.

"Excellent," says Ms. Adams as she quickly scans my paperwork. "We are so happy to have you here, Roonie. I think you will enjoy your time at the hospital. We will set up a volunteer orientation session, but for today you can just familiarize yourself with your area. When you come for your volunteer sessions, always check in at this desk first. Then head up to the fifth floor.

The person on duty at the nursing station will give you your duties for the day. Nothing too difficult, don't worry. In fact, your main job is to cheer up the patients while they are staying in the hospital. It's an important role." She hands the clipboard to the receptionist. "Oh, and when you leave, remember to check in at the desk again so they can log your hours. We will provide a summary for your school at the end of the semester. Does that all sound okay?"

"Sure," I answer. But I didn't hear much after she mentioned the *nursing* station! I hope I don't have to do anything like draw blood! I am pretty laid back, except when it comes to three things—blood, puke and brussels sprouts!

"Here's your badge. You will need to wear it at all times, every time you volunteer."

The badge is plain and simple. It says *Hospital Volunteer*. I pin it to my sweatshirt. I am wearing the orange-and black-sweatshirt that has a picture of Jay-Z on the front. Along with Drake, he's one of my favorite hip-hop artists. Ms. Adams looks me up and down. I can tell she does not approve of my shirt. I guess I should remember to wear something dressier next time.

"Do you have any questions?"

Of course, my main question is, What the heck *is* the geriatric wing? But I don't want to look foolish. So I just shake my head.

"Okay then. Just take the elevator up to the fifth floor. When you step out, turn left. The nursing station is right there. I believe Patricia is on today. She'll get you set up with your duties. Nice to have you with us, Roonie."

I pull my water bottle out of my pack and swig several deep gulps.

The hospital is dry, and still not knowing what I'm going to be doing has definitely raised my stress level.

I climb into the elevator car when it arrives. A man in light blue pants and a matching blue shirt gets in with me. He pushes the button for the third floor. Right. I need to push the button for the fifth floor. I lean across in front of him to hit the number five. As he steps back to give me room, I manage a small smile.

When he gets off the elevator, I let out a deep breath. In moments I will know what my volunteer assignment will look like. I think of Kira. She is probably checking out the cute dudes dancing at the studio. How did she get so lucky? She promised me she will check out as many new moves as she can so that we can add them to our dance. I can't wait to get out of here and back to practicing our hip-hop routine. I look at my watch—three thirty. I have to stay for at least an hour. As the elevator doors open, all I can think about is that sixty minutes is a long time.

Chapter Four

I slowly step out of the elevator. A man in the same blue outfit as the guy in the elevator nearly bumps into me. He's pushing an old lady on a bed with wheels. She reaches out to me as they pass, her dry, wrinkled hand grasping at my arm. The man nudges me out of the way so he can get into the elevator before the door closes. The woman moans.

I feel like I just walked into a zombie movie. I tug at my sweatshirt.

As I head to the desk, I see a woman in a white nursing outfit behind the counter. I can see by her name tag that she is Patricia. She's the person I need to connect with. But my feet won't move closer to the counter, and my mouth doesn't seem to want to spit out any words. I stand there for a few minutes. Finally, Patricia looks up and sees me. Her brown eyes are warm. She smiles.

"You must be our new volunteer. It's been a long time since we've had any volunteers up here. And an even longer time since we've had anyone your age. I am excited. It's a great way to introduce a young person to the life of a hospital. So do you want to be a doctor or a nurse?"

"Hi. I…well…I like to dance." OMG. How lame is that response? "What I mean is…I like to dance and wanted to volunteer at our local dance studio. But I kind of missed the deadline for handing in my application." I try to laugh, hoping she finds me charming.

Patricia's smile gets bigger. "Not to worry. We will try not to scare you off then! Why don't we start out slow? You can begin with the magazines. You see that rolling shelf over there?" My eyes follow her pointing finger to a small gray cart piled high with books and magazines. I nod while she continues. "You can go room to room and ask the patients if they would like anything to read. It's a great way to introduce yourself too. I find it helps if you spend a few moments connecting with each of the patients. Most of them love getting visitors. And they won't bite—I promise!"

I feel my whole body relax. I can totally handle giving magazines out to people. No big deal. "Sounds good," I say. "So are these people sick or recovering from surgeries or broken bones or what?"

"Well, this is the geriatric ward. This is where senior citizens get appropriate support for their health issues. Those issues vary from patient to patient." Patricia smiles and turns back to the computer. "Off you go then. We'll see you back here in an hour."

Senior citizens. Old people who have issues. Like my gram.

I turn around and march right back to the elevator. I push the Down button over and over, until it beeps and the door opens. As I step in, I look back. Patricia is watching me. I'm sure she must be disappointed. I haven't even give the position a chance. But the panic racing through my body makes it hard to think clearly.

The door closes. I slump against the wall of the elevator. On the third floor a couple gets on. They have just been visiting their mom and clearly don't want to leave.

"I wish I could stay with her all day," says the man.

"She must feel so lonely," says the woman.

I think about Gram. She is alone most of the time at the seniors' home. Mom and Dad both work, and Jordan and I are at school. Dad usually goes to see her after work a few times during the week, but the whole family only visits on Sundays. The last time I visited was so long ago. I can't even remember what Gram and I did.

My chest heaves as we reach the main floor.

Instead of leaving the elevator, I step back as new people get on. With my elbow, I nudge a dude who is invading my personal space. He's not much older than me. He gets out at the fourth floor, but not before turning around and giving me an evil glare. I want to stick out my tongue at him, but don't want to seem juvenile. So I just raise my eyebrows and shrug.

The next floor is my stop. As I step out, Patricia looks up and smiles. I manage to give a weak smile back. I grab the gray cart and then head down the hall to the left. The first room I enter smells funny. I try not to imagine what is causing the odor. The old man in the first bed is asleep, snoring loudly. The second bed is empty, but the sheets and blankets are pulled back. Maybe the person will want something to read when they return. I plop a *Popular Mechanics* on the pillow.

I continue down the hall to the next room. I have to plug my nose this time. It smells like someone peed the bed. An elderly woman in one of the beds is crumpled up in the sheets. Her eyes are open, but she is just staring at the ceiling. I can't tell if she is alive. She doesn't blink and doesn't look my way when the wheels of the cart squeak.

I rush out of the room so fast, I bang the cart against the door. This scares the person in the other bed, who moans as if in severe pain or scared to death. I don't wait to find out. I scramble out of there and almost run into a man in the hall who is pushing a walker. His wrinkled butt is showing. I avert my eyes and head for the next room so I don't have to see him shuffle down the hall.

The only thing I notice before I roll into the next room is that the sign on the door says *ROOM 555*.

Chapter Five

As my heart rate slows down, I scan the room. I see two people in their beds. The bathroom door is propped open, and beyond it I spot a chair and table with flowers and cards. The curtains are open, letting light into the room. I guess that's why the last room scared me so much. The curtains were closed, and it was dark. This room almost seems welcoming.

I push the cart in and notice that the woman in the first bed is doing some kind of exercise with her arms. She holds them at chest level and lets them sway out to one side and then across to the other. She sees me and drops her arms.

"Sorry," I say. "I didn't mean to startle you."

"Oh, you didn't startle me. I'm just not ready to show off my dance moves yet."

"Dance moves?" I ask as I roll the cart up beside her bed.

She grins and leans toward me, as though she has a deep secret to share. "Yes. The ladies and I are getting ready for our Winter Showcase, and I don't want to let them down. I plan to be ready to dance, even if it kills me." Then she laughs again. I notice that the lower part of her left leg is not covered by a blanket. It's wrapped in a brace.

Her ankle looks swollen and red. She tries to lift her leg and winces with pain.

"Are you okay?" I ask.

"Shush. Of course I'm okay. Didn't I just say I have some pretty hot dance moves to work on?"

I don't have the heart to tell her that the swaying she was doing did not look like any dance moves I have ever seen. She motions for me to come even closer. Her breath smells like fruit. There's a glass of cranberry juice on her bedside table.

"Did you see my physio therapist out there? I've been buzzing for him all day. They wrapped my ankle all wrong again. Look at it. It shouldn't be like that." It does look like the part of the brace around the ankle is twisted in an awkward way.

"He says he used to be a ballet dancer," the woman adds. "But don't tell anyone. I think it's a secret." She grins again and then points at my cart. "What have you got there? Any poetry? Anything other than how-to books?"

I haven't really looked at the cart's contents yet, so I can't answer. I survey the top shelf. A few fashion and recipe magazines, but others are definitely the how-to type. The books on the lower shelf of the cart don't look that interesting either.

"Sorry, I don't think there's much here that would be interesting for you." I think we have some old magazines in our garage she might like. I will try to remember to bring them in next time. "What kind of dance were you doing just now?" I ask.

"Ah, you liked it, didn't you?"

I shrug.

"It's belly dancing. I've been doing it for years. And a smashed ankle isn't going to stop me now." She moves her leg like she is going to do a dance move but cringes with pain and rolls her head back down to her pillow. She waves me away. I don't know what to say.

The second bed has another woman, curled up asleep. There is a book open on her chest. It looks like it's about World War II.

"I…well…I have to go now. I hope… you feel better."

As I leave the room, I look at the names listed near the doorway. The dancing woman is either Jasmine or Yolanda. I finish my volunteer duties and head home.

"Mom, do you remember where that pile of old magazines is? I couldn't see them in the garage."

"Oh, I think your dad finally recycled them. Why? School project?"

"No, my volunteer thing. Do we have any books of poetry?"

"Not here, but there are plenty at work. Do you want me to pick up anything in particular?"

"Nope. Just anything that has to do with poetry. Thanks." My mom works at the library, so she has access to pretty much anything. I thought about asking her to get a book on belly dancing but then decided it would be way faster to look it up on the internet. So after dinner I clear the table and do the dishes, then head to my room. Instead of working on my dance moves, I get sucked into belly-dance sites.

I watch several clips on YouTube. Women in bright costumes are swaying their hips and doing wave movements with their arms. Sometimes they look like a moving ocean. Other times, when they raise their arms above their heads, they look like a live snake or a bird. The dancers do a lot of flicks and kicks with their legs. I think about the lady in room 555. How can she possibly do all this with a crushed ankle?

I finally get off the computer and try to work on my routine. But all I can think about is what would happen if I got injured. How would I walk? How would I dance?

Chapter Six

On Wednesday after school I go with Kira to her volunteer session at the dance studio. I thought I would hang out in the reception area until she is done. But when she gets called away for something, I go exploring. I have never taken any formal dance lessons. I mostly watch dance shows on TV and loads of YouTube videos to get ideas. So I am super impressed with what I see through the windows of each studio.

The first one has five little girls and one boy doing ballet. When they slide down into the splits, I have to laugh. That move took me a long time to master because I'm not naturally flexible. I had to train my muscles. These kids do it without even thinking about it.

The next room is full of a bunch of girls about my age. The sign on the door says *Jazz*. I watch the girls do a lot of complicated steps with jumps and raised arms. They look like they're enjoying moving to the music, but it's not really my thing.

The last room has two guys and a girl doing hip hop. I am mesmerized by them. There are at least three moves I have never seen before. I try to copy them as they repeat their steps over and over.

"Cool," says Kira. She's come to join me at the window.

"Do you think we can add something like that to our routine?" I ask.

"We can try! How about we meet tomorrow after school?"

"Can't. Have to do my volunteer hours."

"Oh, right. Well, we'll find a time. But I better get back to my shift. See you at school tomorrow?"

"Sure," I answer. I'm not really ready to leave the studio yet, but I don't want Kira to get in trouble. So I head home and try to recreate the moves I saw in the studio. They are like a mix of stop-and-drops, with big arm crosses. But they are super-fluid moves. When I watched the girl at the studio do it, her back was arched and her head was closer to the floor. I try three times and lose my balance and fall to the floor every time. This is going to take some work!

The next morning I remind Mom that I have my volunteer shift at the hospital after school.

"Oh, right! I checked out a few books for you to take with you. But you are responsible for returning them by the due date."

"Okay, Mom. What did you get?"

"Well, I wasn't sure what you wanted, so I chose a few different ones. John Keats, Samuel Taylor Coleridge, Robert Frost. How's that sound?"

"Great, thanks," I say as she digs out the books from her library bag. I've never heard of any of the poets, but I hope the woman in room 555 has. I look at the stack in my arms. I realize there are four books. One is about Emily Carr. She's a painter.

"Mom, why'd you get this one?"

"Oh, you know how your Gram loved painting? Well, one of her favorite artists is Emily Carr. I thought you might like to read up on her so you two have something to talk about. What do you think? Maybe you can join us this Sunday?"

I don't know why the idea freaks me out so much. I don't answer Mom. I jump up from the table, grabbing the poetry books and stuffing them in my backpack. I swing the pack over my shoulder and head for the door. I hear Mom call out, "Have a great day!"

I still don't reply. I'm worried that if I do, all the words in my head will come flying out. I want to tell my mom I can't go see Gram on Sunday. I don't think I could handle it if Gram doesn't remember me. I don't think I can handle watching Gram get weaker and weaker.

Of course, it's pouring rain outside. At least it makes the tears running down my face less obvious. When I get to school, I keep my mind off Gram by really paying attention in my classes. Something I never do.

I'm surprised to realize I'm looking forward to heading to the hospital for my shift. I hope the woman in room 555 likes the books I'm bringing for her. We have to write about our volunteer experiences, so I have decided I will focus on her.

I don't bother with the cart when I step off the elevator. I just head straight to room 555.

Chapter Seven

The two women are chatting with each other as I enter the room. The first time I met her, the belly dancer's hair was a mess. This time she is sitting up in bed, and her blond hair is curled. She has some light makeup on, almost as if she was expecting a special visitor.

"Oh, hello again," she says. "I was just talking with Yolanda. Did you know she was a bomb girl during the war? She worked in Ontario with explosives. Such a dangerous job! Isn't that amazing?"

I guess it is pretty cool. But I don't say that—I just nod.

The woman pats her bed for me to come closer. "I'm Jasmine," she says. "I didn't catch your name last time."

"My name is Roonie, short for Macaroon. My grandmother gave me that nickname, and it stuck."

"Roonie! I love it. And I'd like to meet this lady. She sounds pretty smart!"

I smile at Jasmine's words, but my heart sinks. She can't meet Gram. Gram is in the care home. Jasmine doesn't look too mobile right now, either. But somehow, her words comfort me. She is right. She and Gram would probably get along. She seems as youthful as my gram was before she got sick.

"And what do you have there?" Jasmine asks, looking at the books tucked under my arm.

I hand her the three books of poetry. She lights up. "Ah, Coleridge is one of my favorites. How did you know?"

"I didn't. My mom picked them up at the library. I have to return them or she will be after me. So please don't lose them."

"Oh, I won't. They are precious books, and I will take care of them. Thank you for doing this, Roonie." Jasmine turns to the bomb girl. "Yolanda, isn't she a good girl?"

I cringe at the words. Yolanda nods.

"So, Roonie, tell me more about yourself. What do you like to do? What are you passionate about? What makes you happiest?"

I kind of love her questions. They allow me to go right to my favorite thing. "Well, I am really into hip-hop dancing."

To demonstrate, I do a jolting chest pop. I think it is the best one I have done yet. Too bad it wasn't caught on camera.

"Hmmm," Jasmine says. "That looks very similar to something belly dancers do. Can you show me again? And what other kinds of moves do you do in hip hop?"

"Well, there are a lot of freestyle moves, so you can't really pin it down to one shape or one move."

"Kind of like poetry," says Jasmine. "One dance might be like free verse and another like a Shakespearean sonnet. Would you say the style closest to your dance moves might be like… slam poetry?"

Wow. I did not expect someone of this woman's age to be so cool. I do a few shuffle-slide steps while pushing my arms down to the floor. When I look up, Jasmine is grinning.

She sits up in her bed and tries the same arm moves. I want to laugh, because she actually isn't bad. But I don't want her to think I'm laughing at her, so I just smile. "Pretty good," I say.

"Well, maybe I should add that move to my daily routine! I have been doing my dance moves every day. Well, at least the upper-body motions. I am still struggling with my leg."

I look at her leg and am happy to see that the brace has been adjusted and is on properly now.

"My therapist told me today that if I don't feel any pain, there won't be any gain. So he made me do my leg lifts with weights on. Well, look at how much my ankle has swollen now!"

Yikes. Her ankle looks like a blood orange sticking out through the hole in the brace. Jasmine lifts the blanket and shows me the bruises all down her lower leg.

"That's not right," I say. "Can't you tell them it hurts?"

"Well, I just want to get better and go home soon."

"I understand," I say. "I hear the food isn't so great."

"No, it isn't. And it's hard to sleep at night..." Jasmine drops her voice down to a whisper. "Yolanda snores. A lot!"

I chuckle. I can relate. When we go camping in the summer in our tent trailer, I just about die. My dad snores so loudly, I am sure he keeps the whole campground awake.

"Why can't you go home now?"

"I live down by the water, and there are too many stairs to climb to get to my house. And inside my home, I have to be able to manage three *more* sets of stairs. My bedroom is on the third floor. I can't manage that right now, and I live by myself."

I feel a lump fill my throat, and it becomes tough to swallow. I would not want to be alone with a smashed ankle and hundreds of stairs to climb.

"Can't you get someone to help you?"

"Well, I need to heal first. But I am making plans to move to another place soon. The only bad thing about that is, I won't be able to see you anymore, Roonie."

"*Aww*. This is only our second time hanging out. But it does seem like we've known each other for longer."

"Enough of the mushy stuff," Jasmine says. "Let me tell you about something funny that happened today."

Just then a nurse comes. She's here for Yolanda. She looks at my badge and rolls the bed out into the hall. She puts her hand on my shoulder and says, "Thank you."

"Okay, are you ready for my story?" asks Jasmine.

"Yup, but hang on one second." I follow the nurse out and ask if I can get Jasmine an ice pack for her foot. The nurse points me in the direction of a small room. I pull an ice pack out of the freezer. When I give it to Jasmine, she smiles and nods for me to pull up a chair beside her bed. I slide it over and plop into it.

"So," she begins. "Today I tried to shower on my own. Picture this…"

I don't want to picture an older person showering! Actually, I don't want to picture *anyone* showering.

Jasmine continues, "I am standing in this large, open shower space. It's large enough that you could be in there with a wheelchair. I don't have a wheelchair, but I used my crutches to get into it. So with my injured foot raised, I am leaning against the cold wall for balance while the warm water shoots down on me. The shower head is attached to a long hose, which I have in my hand. Well, trying to balance on one leg and shampoo one's hair is no easy task. Before I know it, the shower head slips from my hand and comes alive! It whips around the shower room like a large snake. I can't catch it and still keep my balance. The shower hose twists and curves and water is flying everywhere."

I can totally picture the scene, and I begin to laugh. She joins me. Her laugh reminds me of Gram's. "How did you finally get a hold of the hose?"

"Unfortunately, I had to call for help. It was a long time before anyone came. By then I was drenched and shivering from the cold."

That doesn't seem so funny. I wish someone had come to help Jasmine sooner. Before I can express my concern, an orderly with a cart full of tea and cookies arrives. Jasmine takes a tea, with cream, and asks for two chocolate-chip cookies. As soon as the orderly leaves, she hands the cookies to me. We sit quietly for a few more minutes until I realize I should probably visit some other rooms before my shift ends. I excuse myself and say goodbye.

I am already looking forward to my shift next week.

Chapter Eight

Mom is making dinner when I get home. She seems quiet. She doesn't even ask how Jasmine liked the poetry books. I can smell the butter chicken that has been simmering in the slow cooker all day. Rice is cooking in the steamer, and some vegetables are in a pot on the stove. Dad flies in the door and without even a "Hi," blurts out, "So what happened?"

"Well, they say she fell out of her wheelchair. How can that happen?"

"Are you talking about Gram?" asks Jordan. He is sitting at the table, playing a game on his iPad.

"Yes, son." Mom nods for me to grab the stack of plates and set the table. Dad paces.

"Gram had a fall?" I ask.

Jordan stares me down. "Like you care."

I have the urge to crack a plate over his head.

"Easy...easy," says my dad, pushing his arms down to indicate I should be calm. I place the last plate in front of my brother and glare at him.

"So she fell out of her wheelchair. But is she okay?" Dad's voice is kind of hollow. I know that means he's scared.

"They told me she's bruised, but, thankfully, nothing is broken. It does seem to have set her back emotionally though. They say she seems more 'inside herself' now," says my mom. "Let's all go tomorrow for a visit. I think having *everyone* there will really perk her up. She needs that right now." Mom puts her hand over Dad's.

As Dad spoons some butter chicken over his rice, he turns to me. "You'll come, right?"

I stammer out an answer. "I…I have…I have to…I don't know." I can't make eye contact with anyone at the table. I am so mad at myself. I can't even summon the courage to say whether I will go or not. We finish dinner in silence, and then I head to my room. I pull out my phone and scroll through tons of old photos of me and Gram— photos of her paintings, pictures of spaghetti and meatballs, pictures of macaroons, pictures of all the other things she used to make. I look at the painting on the wall. It's a painting of me that Gram did when I was ten.

The tears come fast, and I can't stop them. I flop onto my bed and bury my face in my pillow. Sobs rack my body. I guess I'm crying so loudly that I don't hear the door open. I feel a hand on my back and turn to see my mom sitting on the edge of my bed. She leans in to hug me, and I let her.

"Mom, I'm just scared."

"Honey, we all are. It's hard to think about losing someone you love. I lost both my mom and dad when I was young, and I never really got over it. I'm sorry I haven't been more sensitive to what you are going through. But it would be really great if you could find the courage to be there for Gram. If you want me to, I will hold your hand, stand beside you, whatever you need. Roonie, she loves you so much. I really hope you can find your way."

I don't respond, but we stay hugging for a few moments. Then Mom tells me she made me a cup of hot chocolate with tiny marshmallows on top, the way I like it. I go downstairs and curl up on the couch, pulling the blanket around me like a cocoon. The hot chocolate is soothing, and its warmth makes me drowsy. Before I know it, my dad is gently shaking my arm.

"Come on, sleepyhead. It's late."

I trudge back up to my bedroom. I can feel sleep overtaking me before my head even hits the pillow. But sometime in the middle of the night, I wake up drenched in sweat. I had a terrible nightmare about our dog, Skip. I dreamed that we lost him, and he never came back. But I can see him curled up in my blankets at the foot of my bed, where he always spends the night.

When I was about five years old, we really did lose Skip for the whole day.

He was just a pup. I was so worried about him. A nice neighbor came over after dinner with Skip in her arms. He had somehow gotten locked in her garage all day.

I call Skip up so I can pet him. But I am too restless and can't get comfortable. Skip heads back to the foot of the bed and closes his eyes. I have trouble falling back to sleep. The last thing on my mind as I finally doze off is that if we lose Gram, nothing will be the same.

The next day after dinner, Mom and Dad are at the front door putting their coats and boots on. It is raining again. Really raining, like a monsoon.

"So," says my brother. "Are you coming or not?"

"Look," I say. "I really was planning to come. But none of you know how tough eighth grade is. I'm not used to this much homework." I look at my mom and dad, and I know they believe me. I really am struggling at school.

Jordan snorts. "But it's Friday. You have all weekend to do your schoolwork. And like you—"

"Well," interrupts Dad. "I know the volunteering you're doing at the hospital is for school, so you can continue with that. But if you're having as much trouble as you say, then maybe you shouldn't be entering this dance competition. I know that takes up a lot of your time with practicing and rehearsing. Why don't you leave the competition until next year, when you don't have so much on your plate?"

Mom jumps in. "Besides, think of how you'll feel if we lose Gram and you didn't take the time to be with her."

"*Joyce*." My dad's voice is low, and his eyes well up with water.

"I'm sorry, dear." Mom puts her arm around Dad.

Without thinking, I blurt out, "I'm not quitting the dance competition!"

Dad shakes his head and turns. "I'll be at the car waiting for anyone who plans on joining us. But you better hurry. My patience just ran out." He heads out the door.

"I'll come next time, Mom," I say. "I promise."

Mom shakes her head and follows my dad. Jordan doesn't look at me as he closes the door behind him. Moments later I hear the car pull out of the driveway and roar off down the street. I slump to the floor.

Why am I so scared?

I go up to my room, hoping to practice my hip-hop routine and forget what just happened. There's no way Dad can make me drop the competition now. It's the only thing holding me together.

But as I try some moves, I realize my heart is not in it. I would go see Jasmine at the hospital, but I haven't checked to see if it's okay for me to go there outside of my volunteer hours. It's probably too late anyway, and Jasmine's not expecting me. Or maybe I'm just stalling? I pick up my phone and call Kira. But before she can answer, I disconnect the call.

I look out the window at the rain. All I can think about is what Mom and Dad said. Gram's fall set her back. She needs some family time to help her regain her strength. I think of Jasmine with her broken ankle and of how much pain she is in. About how just having me stand by her bed seemed to make her feel better.

Will that be enough for my grandma? Can I really make a difference?

I throw on my rain gear and run to the garage. I grab my bike and pedal hard. It's a ten-minute drive to the care home, but on my bike it takes a lot longer. Thankfully, it's mostly downhill, so I coast a lot. The rain splashes up my back, and I'm wet everywhere. But when I arrive at the care home, I can't find the courage to go in the front door. It would be warm and dry inside. I sneak around the back. I know approximately where Gram's room is. I peek in a few windows until I find hers.

Jordan is sitting on the bed, holding Gram's hand. He doesn't see me. Jordan is only eleven. How is he so brave? If my little brother can do it... Just then Dad steps into the room. I guess he was out in the hall, probably getting coffee. Before he can look my way, I duck. Keeping low, I run back to the front entrance and grab my bike. I start the hard trek home.

It's like I'm paralyzed. Like I can do everything else in my life right now except the one thing that's most important. I can't get to Gram. I can't make myself visit her, and I don't understand why.

Chapter Nine

On Sunday everyone goes to visit
Gram again. I stay home and finish all
my homework. I even get a head start
on some upcoming projects. This is so
not me! Kira calls and wants to practice
our routine, but I brush her off. Instead
I spend a lot of time looking at old
photos and tracing my finger around
Gram's paintings.

All through dinner, they talk about Gram. I am not allowed to bring headphones to the table, but I am still able to tune them out. I'm not hungry. After watching me play with my dinner for twenty minutes, Mom says I can clear my plate and go to my room. I don't even argue.

At school the next day, I feel like I am not really there. Kira catches up to me as the final bell rings for the day. "What's up?"

"I don't know. This whole thing with my grandma has me cramped up. I can't even dance."

"Well, you better get uncramped, because the competition is Saturday! Do you want to blow it off?"

"Are you crazy? Of course not! Let's go to the gym right now and practice. I heard there aren't any basketball games today, so the gym should be free."

"Now that's what I'm talking about," says Kira. She links her arm with mine, and we head to the gym.

A group of students that look like tenth graders are using the stage for their own dance routine. That means we will have to stay on the floor area of the gym. It's fine—there's room for all of us. As Kira and I warm up our bodies to get ready to dance, I watch the other group.

"Hey, wait a minute!" I march toward the stage. "That's our routine." Almost all of the moves are similar to mine. A few are in a different order, but the routine looks almost identical to ours.

"Are you saying we stole your moves?" asks one of the girls in the group. "We don't even know who you are!" She has her hand on her hip, and the other dancers are now moving to the edge of the stage. It looks like they are preparing for a fight.

Well, if they want a fight, I will give them one! "I got those moves off a show I watch. You copied them."

"Ah...*no*." A dude with major muscles, and attitude to match, has jumped off the stage. "Anyone can use those moves. You think you hold a monopoly on hip hop? Obviously, you were copying the routine from someone else to begin with. So it's pretty stupid to be giving us grief."

"Fine," I say, turning around. I can feel the sting of tears in my eyes and don't want them to know they got to me.

I grab Kira's arm. "Let's get out of here."

"Where are we going?" she asks as I whisk us out of the building.

"To your place." I don't want to be home with Mom and her guilt trips.

At Kira's house we gobble up some chips before starting into our routine. I'm still mad that another group has our moves. There isn't much time to come up with a new routine. I pull out my phone and do a search. I find some grooves similar to the ones I saw the teens doing at the dance studio.

"Here, watch this." I hand Kira my phone as I begin practicing the new steps. The last time I tried them at home, I kept losing my balance. But today the moves come naturally.

Kira gives it a try. She falls every time. Forgetting that I fell lots of times too, I begin to lose patience. I am worried there is no way we'll be ready for the competition. "Hey, *you* were the one who said we need to practice," I snap. "*You* wanted to sign up for the competition. Now it's like you don't even care if we win or lose!" Kira falls again and throws her arms up in the air. "Maybe I should go back to a solo act?" I add.

"Fine!" she snaps back. "*You* didn't want to practice all weekend and wouldn't say why. But, of course, this is all *my* fault. If being in the competition means putting up with all this crap, I'd rather not be a part of it."

Kira walks to her bedroom door and holds it open for me.

I'm shocked that things have fallen apart so fast. I know I'm in the wrong, but I blast out of Kira's room and don't look back. I run all the way home and head straight to my bedroom. Maybe I *am* better off doing a solo act!

I limber up in front of the mirror and then try popping. I get the moves right on my first try. Maybe anger and adrenaline are fueling my dance moves? They are pretty tight! Then I add the hip-hop moves I copied from the teens at the studio. I try a few ideas from the internet, especially some isolations. Everything I try works brilliantly.

Then, just as I pull it all together, Mom calls up the stairs that it is time for dinner. I miss a few key steps and lose my balance. I holler back that I will be down in a few minutes. I try the full routine. Mom calls again, and I lose my focus and flub a few moves.

I start the routine over. I hear Jordan coming up the stairs to get me. I mess up the opening of the routine. Now, instead of my anger making my moves sharper and tighter, I am having trouble concentrating. I see Kira's face as I left her bedroom. She didn't look as mad as her words sounded. Instead, her shoulders were slumped and she was looking down at the floor.

She looked disappointed in me.

Chapter Ten

It's Tuesday, and I'm at the hospital. As I step off the elevator, I can see that a new nurse is at the counter. I introduce myself and explain why I am here. She doesn't look up from her work, doesn't even acknowledge me. I'm already stressed enough, and this just adds to it. I think about just going home, but there is too much stress there too. So I head for room 555.

As I enter the room, Jasmine smiles and immediately starts talking.

"'The Rime of the Ancient Mariner,'" she says. "Now there's a poem."

I don't have a clue what she is talking about.

My face must make that clear. Jasmine holds up one of the books I brought her. "It's a poem Samuel Taylor Coleridge wrote in 1798. It's about an old seaman and an albatross," she says.

Okay. I get that this Coleridge guy wrote poems. I get that this one was written a very long time ago. And it's about some dude who's a sailor. But what the heck is an albatross?

Jasmine motions for me to sit down by the bed. I didn't ask that question out loud, but she answers me.

"An albatross is a very large seabird. It looks a bit like a seagull. It has come to symbolize a great burden of guilt or regret."

I shake my head, still confused.

Jasmine continues. "In the poem, the main character kills the albatross that has been following their ship. Since it's supposed to be a sign of good luck, the rest of the crew are so mad that they make him wear it around his neck as punishment."

"Yuck! You mean like a scarf? But it's really a dead bird?"

"Yes. And sometimes that's what it can feel like when you're feeling guilty about something. Like you're weighed down. But enough of that," she says, piling the three books together and handing them to me. "Thank you so much for bringing me these books. I sure appreciated being able to borrow them."

I don't really hear her last words, because I'm kind of freaked out. It's like she has read my mind. Like she can hear my thoughts. I mean, out of all the poems that must be in the books I gave her, what are the chances of her picking *that* poem to share with me? Does she know what I'm feeling? Maybe she can help me sort through my confusion. "Um, maybe you already know this, but I wasn't even planning on coming today. I haven't had a good week so far."

Jasmine nods, like she wants me to go on.

"It's just," I begin, "it's just…" And then all my words come. I tell her about Dad saying I shouldn't do the dance competition, but that I plan to do it anyway. I tell her about the other group stealing our moves. About how I kind of exploded on Kira and kicked her off our team.

"It's never easy," says Jasmine. "Just one thing can weigh us down with worry, stress…"

"And guilt or regret," I add.

"Yes…and guilt or regret. All that worry and stress make it harder to do the right thing. It may even affect the things we love to do."

"But what should I do next? The thing I want most is to dance, and now I'm failing at that too."

Jasmine sways and rolls her arms across her chest in a belly-dance move. She says, "I don't think you could ever fail at dance. For you and me, dance is in our blood. But something else is getting in your way. Something is preventing you from enjoying what you love."

That's for sure. I don't say it out loud.

I look at Jasmine. Even with her bashed-up ankle, she's still dancing in her hospital bed and getting ready for her big show. She is not letting anything stop her. I know what is stopping me from getting my routine down. I feel guilty about not seeing Gram. And now

I also feel terrible about how I treated Kira.

I look at my reflection in the small mirror above the sink by Jasmine's bed. I can almost see the guilt and regret hanging around my neck. "So how do I get rid of the scarf?"

"Well…" Jasmine rubs her chin as she smiles at me. "You fix what needs fixing! And then you eat Jell-O." She offers me the red wiggling dessert sitting on her lunch tray.

I gobble it down while looking at the other items on her tray. In the middle slot is a strange square block of food. "What is *that*?" I ask.

"I have no idea. That's why I didn't eat it! Mystery loaf."

"Well," I say, "I think it looks like SpongeBob SquarePants."

And just like that, we are both laughing hysterically. I'm amazed Jasmine even knows who SpongeBob

SquarePants is! It feels good to release all this negative energy.

I guess we are too loud, because the nurse on duty comes into the room and tells me to move it along, that I am not there to spend all my time with one patient. Jasmine apologizes for getting me in trouble and says goodbye.

I visit other rooms for the rest of the hour. But I have too much on my mind to talk with anyone else.

Chapter Eleven

I have another volunteer shift the next day. I drag my feet down to room 555. Nothing much has changed, and I know Jasmine is going to give me heck for not dealing with my albatross.

The competition is on Saturday. The school decided to hold it on the weekend because there were so many dance routines entered in the contest. They could not get through them all in one afternoon of school. My dad hasn't said any more about me dropping it, but I haven't seen him that much either. He's mostly spending time with Gram. I am worried I won't be ready for the competition, even though it's just my act now. I'm having trouble hammering out a new routine. I want to stand out. I need to win.

As I enter Jasmine's room, I freeze. The bed is empty. There are no blankets or sheets. Her belongings are all gone. Even my chair isn't there. I drop to the floor.

I think about our last conversation. She didn't say anything about moving back into her house. I was pretty sure she'd be here for a while. How can she possibly go up three flights of stairs on crutches?

Then I think of worse things. What if something else happened to her? What if…

Suddenly I am shaking. I can't catch my breath. This is exactly how I feel when I think about visiting Gram. I just want to run away. So what if I don't finish my volunteer hours? I can do them next year. I even tell myself it won't matter if I miss the competition.

But then I think about how strong Jasmine looked the last time I saw her. How she was getting ready for her Winter Showcase.

She has to be okay! I dig deep to make myself get up off the floor and go to the nurse's station. Thankfully, Patricia is there, standing by the counter.

"What's wrong, Roonie?"

"I…it's just…Jasmine. She's not in her room. Where is she? Did she go home? Did she…?" I can't say the last word.

I hope Patricia is not about to tell me something terrible has happened to my friend. A tear rolls down my cheek.

"Oh," Patricia says, putting her hand on my shoulder, "I'm so sorry we made you worry about Jasmine."

"What happened to her?"

"She's perfectly fine. Well, not fine, given her broken ankle. But nothing else is seriously wrong. We moved her up to the sixth floor this morning. She'll be transferred to a care facility soon, until she is mobile enough to go home."

"Sixth floor! But I'm not assigned to that floor. How will I visit her? What do I do?"

"I am glad to hear that you connected so well with one of our patients. Thank you, Roonie, for putting so much of yourself into your volunteer time here at the hospital. Who knows—maybe we'll make a doctor or nurse out of you yet!" She smiles and stands. A beep goes off, and she excuses herself. As she leaves, she adds, "It's totally fine for you to visit the sixth floor. Why don't you spend twenty minutes taking care of the folks here and then head up to see Jasmine? She's in room 624."

"Thank you," I say. I'm so relieved my friend is okay!

After giving everyone on the fifth floor their reading materials for the day, I take the stairs to the sixth floor. It smells better up here. A nurse behind the counter asks who I am planning to visit. She directs me down the hall to the right. "Third door," she says.

There is Jasmine, sitting up in bed, surrounded by papers. She smiles as I enter and says, "Glad you tracked me down. Good detective work, Roonie! I'm in need of some help."

She holds up one piece of paper. "It's so gray in the hospital. It's so boring and frustrating and full of pain. I didn't think there was any way I could feel creative. But your visits, and the new dance moves you've shown me, seem to have sparked something. Check it out. I wrote a poem!"

The papers have scribbles on them that are hard to decipher. But clearly, they mean something to Jasmine.

Jasmine looks at me, her blue eyes soft and full of sympathy. She pats the bed, so I move in closer.

"How are things with you? Did you work things out with Kira?"

"Well, I haven't seen her yet. What if she doesn't forgive me for being such a jerk?"

"Friends appreciate someone who can take responsibility for their actions. Besides, she is probably missing you as much as you are missing her. And is that all that is troubling you?"

"Well, my mom and I talked, and I felt better at first, but now I feel worse."

"What did you talk about?"

"Losing people."

"Who did you lose?" Jasmine asks gently.

I forgot that I haven't told her about Gram. "Nobody, yet."

"So your talk with your mom didn't really help that much?"

"No. What's happening isn't like losing your keys or your homework... because..."

"Because the idea of *losing* someone doesn't make sense for what you see happening in your life right now."

"Yeah," I say, rolling my sleeve across my eyes. "When a person is *gone*, they aren't here anymore. I haven't *lost* Gram. But I know she's never going to be the same...ever!" Tears stream down my face.

"Oh, Roonie. I am sorry. If it helps, think of things this way," says Jasmine. She looks out the window, where the clouds are parting and a sliver of sunshine is creating a thin line of light across the room. "Yes, sometimes things change, and that can be really hard. But you will always have your memories. That's what you hold on to—fiercely!"

And in that moment, I know she is right. I have already been storing the good memories these last few weeks so that I can hang on to my grandma. Gram didn't make bombs for the war, and she didn't belly dance. But she loved to paint and cook and was the world's greatest grandma. I have those awesome memories. Even my nickname is a gift I get to keep forever. Suddenly everything is so clear. What I am really losing right now is *time* with Gram.

Talking about this with Jasmine has made me feel lighter somehow. I give her a hug.

"And now, it's time for me to do my afternoon exercises," she says. She waves her arms back and forth like she did the first time I met her. Sitting up straighter in bed, she arches her back so she is curving her head down toward the pillow. She looks like a bridge. Her stomach muscles are wickedly strong. "Not bad for a seventy-four-year-old, hey? Did I tell you I once danced for a pharaoh? It was in the opera *Aida*!"

"You are amazing! And I hope I am that flexible when I'm your age." That's when I realize that the move she just did is very similar to the one I have been working on at home. The one that took me so long to master and that Kira is struggling with now. Maybe I should bring Kira to the hospital so that Jasmine can teach her some moves!

Jasmine calls out the names of her dance moves as she practices them. "Snake arms, rib undulations, rib slides and twists, waterfalls and broken twigs. How am I doing?"

The motions remind me of the ocean. The soft swells and waves. Jasmine's dancing is mesmerizing. Another brain flash! I can use these same moves but add a hip-hop edge to them. Then they will look sharp, like a storm on the ocean. They will be intense—just what my dance needs!

"Hey, Jasmine, I hope you don't mind, but I need to go. I need to get home and add some moves to my choreography. And there's someone I need to call!"

Chapter Twelve

"Hey, Kira," I say as I catch up to her after school. I decided to talk with her in person instead of texting or calling when I got home last night. She's on her way to the dance studio.

"I don't want to be late," she says. There is a frostiness to her tone. She is still mad at me for messing things up with us.

If I am going to fix this, the first thing I need to do is apologize for yelling at her. "Can I walk with you? That way you won't be late."

She shrugs, so I walk quickly to catch up. I want to put my arm through hers, the way we always used to walk home from school. But first I have to make things right. "I totally messed up the other day. I was mad at myself and the dudes that stole our dance moves, and I took it out on you. That wasn't fair. You are a great dancer, and I had just as much trouble as you when I first tried to bend backward. I had no right to criticize your moves."

I have been looking straight ahead as we walk, but now I glance sideways to see Kira's reaction. She is nodding her head up and down.

"Does that mean we're good?" I ask.

"We're good!" she says, grabbing my arm and racing so we can cross while the light is still green. Kira has always been very forgiving and easy to get along with. This was the longest we'd ever gone without talking to each other.

"Yes!" I slap my hands together. "So we only have two days to get our routine down. Do you think we can do it and still be ready by Saturday?"

"Absolutely! Why don't you come with me to the studio right now, so we can squeeze in some practice time and hang out?"

We are actually twenty minutes early for Kira's shift. So I teach Kira the new move I created after seeing Jasmine's ocean arm movements. I add grit to the arm swings and isolate the moves so that they almost look robotic. Kira suggests I do the moves first and lean toward her, and then she'll do the arm pops over my arms. We can't see ourselves in a mirror, but it feels good. And usually when my hip-hop moves feel good, they look good too.

A flurry of people arrives for the next set of classes, and a few parents register their kids for the January sessions. When it's all clear, Kira and I have time to practice two rounds in front of the mirror. The teacher for the hip-hop class walks by on his way into the third studio.

"Hey, I like your back collapse—we call that the 'Matrix.' That's one sick routine."

Good thing I know that *sick* is a compliment!

I read his name tag and say, "Thanks, Jayden."

"Have you guys tried anything like this?" Right in front of us, Jayden does a backflip into the splits and then slides up into a step-touch groove.

"Whoa!" Kira and I exclaim at the same time. She is shaking her head. Like me, she is probably worried about cracking her neck.

"Okay, can you slow-mo that? We have to figure out how to do it without paralyzing ourselves!"

Jayden begins the move again. He doesn't slow it down, because that wouldn't be safe, but he does tell us what he's doing to get his body ready to flip. His students have come out to the hall, and they cheer for him as he finishes the slick moves.

"There you go. Sorry, I have to get to my class now. But good luck with your routine."

"Thanks again," I say. Kira heads back up front to the reception area. I hang back and watch his class for the next fifteen minutes. I can't believe how many great ideas I'm getting.

I say goodbye to Kira and head home. We plan to meet tomorrow morning, half an hour before the bell. We have a forty-minute lunch break to practice some more. Tomorrow after dinner, we will keep on dancing until we get it right. We will be ready for the competition.

Jordan is sitting in the kitchen when I arrive. He's got his homework spread out all over the table.

"Need any help?" I ask.

"Since when is schoolwork your favorite thing?"

"I just thought if it's something I took in my classes, I might remember enough to make it easier for you. What are you working on?"

He shoves his math book my way and bites his nail. I do remember doing fractions. Not fun! I spend the next twenty minutes helping Jordan. When we are done, I ask him if he can do me a favor.

"Maybe. What do you want me to do?" He looks suspicious.

"Well." I take a deep breath. Once I say it out loud, I'm committed. *Yup, I'm doing this!* "Kira and I are still going to do that dance competition," I say quickly.

"I thought Dad banned you!"

"He did, sort of. He was really just trying to help me get my priorities straight. But I have been on top of my homework all week. And Kira and I are working hard to get a routine sorted out and perfected by Saturday."

"So what do you need me for?"

"I'm hoping you will record a video of us doing our routine tomorrow night. When we are ready. What do you say?"

"Why do you need to record yourselves before the competition? Wouldn't it be better to catch the real dance on Saturday?"

"Because I haven't told Mom and Dad I am going to the competition. Not yet. Will you do it? You can use my phone."

"Okay, I guess so. But I don't want to get in trouble." Jordan says.

"You won't. I will tell Mom and Dad everything. After the dance. They won't know you even knew about me going."

It's all coming together. It feels good to be connected with my best friend again. And it feels good not to be fighting with my brother, to actually be able to help each other.

I can't wait to share the video!

Chapter Thirteen

On Friday, Kira and I practice our routine once on the stage at lunch. We pull out mats so we can try the backflips. I get it right the second try. Kira is worried she will fall, so she isn't giving enough push on the take-off to complete the flip.

We go back to the stage after school. Kira wants to practice some more. But I have a shift at the hospital.

"Will you be okay to work on the routine yourself?" I ask.

"Yup. And I will be doing crazy backflips by the time you finish. Where are we going to meet when you are done?"

"Let's go to my place. Jordan said he'll record our routine."

"Cool. Meet you there!"

I run to the hospital. Jasmine is sitting up in her bed on the sixth floor. Her hair is curled, and she's wearing makeup. Her blue eyes sparkle when she sees me.

"So, how did it go?"

"Which part?" I ask.

"Well, whichever part you fixed."

We laugh. I tell her how I apologized to Kira and then show her the routine we worked out. As I finish, Jasmine is already moving her arms in a jerky fashion, trying to copy our isolations and pops.

"Wow! You really pick up choreography fast! How is *your* dance coming along?" I ask.

"Here. I'll show you half of the routine." She shows me the arm movements. Sometimes her arms look like a live snake.

"Why did you say that was only half of the routine?"

"Because the other half is with my legs, and I can't show you that just yet."

Again we laugh. It's always so good to laugh with her.

When it's time for me to head home, Jasmine wishes me luck and makes me promise to come and tell her how it all went.

Friday night Kira and I practice until ten thirty. Jordan films us. It's one of our best efforts, but Kira skips the backflip. She says she will keep trying.

By Saturday morning, we have the complete routine down except for the backflip. I can do it fine, but Kira is still nervous about it. Instead of being mad at her, I tell her how proud I am that she never gave up trying. We decide to adjust the choreography so that when we get to the backflip, she is bending down close to the floor, with her right hand grabbing her chin like she is thinking. I will do the flip over her and land in the splits. Then we will start moving in sync again. We try it twice, and it rocks!

"Ready?" asks the student working the curtain on the stage. The tenth graders we clashed with earlier this week have just left the stage. I have to admit, they were pretty good. We are up next. Through a small gap in the curtain, I can see our parents sitting together. Good thing Dad didn't get too upset this morning when I told him I was still planning on competing. I made sure he knew I was all caught up with my school work. Jordan sits between my parents, grinning up at us. Our names are called, the curtain goes up, and we strike a pose.

The music begins. I feel like I am channeling all my favorite hip-hop dancers—and Jayden from the dance studio. I even feel like Jasmine is dancing along with me. When we arch our backs for the Matrix move, neither one of us falls. The crowd goes crazy. Then, when I do the backflip and Kira hits her position, the audience claps and whistles. Adrenaline fills me up as we take our bows.

There is an eleventh-grade solo act after us that blows me away. The final act is contemporary dance from a twelfth-grade group. They are so amazing, I get goose bumps. Who knew there was so much talent at our school? Either one of the last two acts could take first place.

The judges take a few minutes to decide and then get ready to announce the winners.

I bite my lip and hold hands with Kira. The judges call third place first. It's us!

We fly across the stage. I can see our parents beaming. Someone asks us to stand together with our trophy to get a picture. Second place goes to the eleventh-grade soloist. First place is the twelfth-grade group.

After I come down from the excitement, it occurs to me that if we had stuck with our original dance, we probably wouldn't have finished in the top three. The tenth-grade dancers didn't even place.

After the competition our two families head to the Dairy Queen to celebrate with ice cream. On the way

home I ask my parents if they can drop
me off at the hospital. I tell them there
is something I have to do before supper.

Chapter Fourteen

I run up to Jasmine's room. She is having her dinner, even though it is only four forty-five. It doesn't look like SpongeBob SquarePants, but it doesn't look appealing either. I should have brought her a sundae!

After her last bite, Jasmine pats the bed, and I pull the chair up beside her. "Well," she says, "tell me everything.

How did the dance routine go? More important, how did you feel when you finished?"

"It was awesome! Kira hit every move hard. I didn't fall when I rolled back, and I kept my balance after the backflip. We came in third. But that was okay. The first- and second-place dancers totally deserved their win."

"Congratulations! I would have loved to be there."

"I thought you might feel that way." I pull out my phone. I carefully scroll through videos until I find what I'm looking for.

"Okay, so this isn't the dance we did today, but I got my brother to record our rehearsal dance from last night. Today's was even better because we worked off the audience's energy. They were stoked, so we poured our hearts into the dance. But this one still gives you a pretty good idea of our routine."

As Jasmine watches, her eyes brighten. She smiles and nods at several spots through the two-minute piece. Even her shoulders are bopping to the music by the time the video finishes. She tries a few moves herself, and we both laugh.

"Well done, Roonie! Thank you so much for showing me. But I think there is probably someone else who would love to see this video."

I don't have to ask who she means. I know right away. And she is right.

I lean in and give her a hug. Then I run all the way home.

At the dinner table, I lean over to Jordan. "Will you be going to see Gram tomorrow?"

"Yup. Why? Don't tell me you're actually coming!" He looks at me with his eyebrows raised.

"Yep, I think I will." I turn to my mom. "Do we have the ingredients to make macaroons?"

Dad beams, and Mom puts her hand over his and smiles at me. Jordan clears the dishes while I look up recipes for macaroons. I'm relieved to find they don't look too hard to make.

The next morning, Mom helps me make the cookies. After beating the egg whites and sugar to soft, glossy white peaks, I fold in the coconut. Then we form the little haystacks on the cookie sheet and pop them in the oven.

When they have turned golden brown, I take them out and leave them on top of the stove to cool. I bet they won't be as tasty as Gram's, but I am happy with how they turned out.

I change out of my sweats and put on my dressy jeans with the matching jacket. I come back downstairs and see that Mom has laid out the cookies on a plate Gram gave us for Christmas several years ago. I carefully carry them to the car. Once I am buckled in, the fear of seeing Gram hits me hard. My legs shake all the way to the care home.

I hesitate by the entrance. I know Gram will be happy to see me. And I know that by being with her, I am storing up good memories so I will never *lose* her. But my feet aren't moving. Mom and Dad are already inside.

Jordan is still hanging with me. "Hey, did you bring the video? I bet Gram would love to see it."

"Do you really think so?"

"Duh! You guys were great. Even if you are my sister!"

We laugh and go inside. My dad is smiling and holds his arm out so I can lean into him for support as we head toward Gram's room.

Just like at the hospital, the smells hit me as soon as we head down the hall. It feels like my first volunteer shift at the hospital. But I am more comfortable than I thought I would be—I guess all those hospital visits helped. When we get to her room, everybody falls back so I can enter first with the plate.

"Macaroons from my Roonie!"

I rush to Gram's side. She looks frail, but that grin from ear to ear is all I really see. She isn't mad at me. She pats her cheek so I can give her a kiss, and then she reaches for one of the cookies and takes a bite.

A tear escapes my eye, and I wipe it away before Gram sees it. Dad comes in and hugs his mom, while my mom puts her arm around me.

Later, after talking about the time we went to Disneyland with Gram and she chased Mickey down for a photo, my parents and my brother head for the door. I guess they want to give me some time alone with Gram. Jordan points to my phone as he leaves.

I scroll through the videos to find the dance. I show it to Gram. She cries when it has finished playing. "I wish I could have been there with you," she says. "You sure are a strong dancer. We're both creative, you and I." Gram smiles and looks off into the distance.

She motions for me to move in closer. She whispers, "I love painting, you know. My favorite is the one I painted of you."

I hug her tightly, and when we finally pull apart, our cheeks are wet. "Bye, Gram. I promise I will come visit tomorrow and as often as I can."

Chapter Fifteen

For the past two weeks, I have gone to visit Gram on the weekends. Before I had to return it, I looked through the book about Emily Carr with Gram. We both loved the paintings. My favorite is one called *Totem Walk at Sitka*. Gram's favorite is, of course, one with people, a watercolor. The second part of the title makes me crack up: *London Student Sojourn* (*burning a sock with a spirit lamp*).

Just like at the hospital, there are lots of people at Gram's care home who don't have people to visit with them. It makes me realize how easy it is for me to help, to make someone's day. I decide I will continue volunteering at the hospital, even after my volunteer placement is done.

I've already met a man who told me about his great love and how they met in the war. He showed me pictures of the two of them flying airplanes. I met someone who was a mountain climber, and another person who went on African safaris. So many adventures in each room!

I am staying on top of my homework. Mom and Dad realized after the dance competition that I am really serious about pursuing my passion for dance.

I think Gram talked to them too. I am now registered for the hip-hop session at the dance studio. It looks like Jayden will be my instructor.

Jasmine left the hospital last week because a space opened up in a care facility where she can get support until she's ready to go home. Since it is farther away from my school, I can't visit her on my own. Today my mom is driving me there to see her. Mom says she'll wait in the car.

Mom also picked up some new books of poetry and other titles that Jasmine told me she likes.

My arms are loaded down because we also brought homemade banana bread. Since it is my first time visiting, I have to sign in and tell them who I am visiting before they give me a special code to open the door. I follow the long hallway to Jasmine's room. I hear moans coming from the room to my left. In the room to my right, I see a shriveled body, curled up asleep, while the TV is blaring full blast.

When I finally reach Jasmine, she smiles weakly. She doesn't look as polished as she did when I saw her in the hospital.

"Well, hello, Roonie! Isn't this quite the place?" She yawns. She has bags under her eyes.

"It's nice that you have your own room. It's probably quieter than the hospital."

"Not really. The lady in the next room cries out every night around 2:00 AM. She calls for her husband. Apparently, he passed away years ago. Then she buzzes for the nurses constantly. It's hard to get back to sleep."

The room is large, and her window looks out onto a grassed area with a single tree. Since it snowed yesterday, the ground and the branches of the tree are covered in white. I hand Jasmine the books, and without looking at the titles, she slides them to the other side of her bed. A dresser on the far wall has two cards on it. She motions for me to pour her a glass of water. Then, without being asked, I pull the one chair in the room up beside her bed.

Jasmine does not seem herself.

"You know, I found out the second day I was here that the second floor is where they send people to die. If you don't get better, that is your fate. I don't want to end up on the second floor."

"But you won't," I say. What has happened to the bubbly, larger-than-life Jasmine I know? My voice is louder but also cracks a little as I try to convince her that everything will be okay. "Remember? You have a dance to perform. When is the first show?"

"In a month. I'll never be ready. I'm using a walker now." She points at the gray metal support in the corner of the room. "Have you ever seen a belly dancer using a walker?"

She laughs a little. I join in, picturing a belly dancer rolling her stomach muscles over the bars of a walker.

"Can't you join the other dancers but just stick to the arm movements?"

"I thought of that. I may do it for the first dance. But I really want to be able to complete the full routine."

I know what she means. Dance is something that uses every muscle and all of our limbs. Half a body moving feels like only half a dance. But I can see that Jasmine needs to believe she will be dancing again soon.

I take out my cell phone and pull up the camera. "Let's see what you've got," I say.

"Oh, not yet!" I see a spark returning. Jasmine fiddles with her hair and then sends me to the bathroom to bring her the makeup bag and comb. She fixes herself up and then says, "Okay, let's do this!"

I video her dance moves. She turns her arms up to the sky, then intertwines them as she lowers them to her waist. Her hips move from side to side in the bed. Her smile widens.

I have to go because Mom has an appointment. But I leave Jasmine my cell phone so she can watch her performance over and over again.

The next day I go back to see Jasmine and get my cell phone back. She is dressed up and heading to the lunchroom.

"I'm so glad to see you, Roonie! Please thank your mom for the books. Also, thank you for being just the medicine I needed. I practiced my dance all evening. Our choreographer and dance coach came in to see me this morning. We have a new gig booked for three weeks from today. If I can make it to that one, it will be good practice for our big show."

"Where is the gig?"

"At the Cedars Care Home for Seniors."

"That's where my gram is staying!" I blurt out. "You will finally get to meet each other."

And Gram and I will have front-row seats to the show.

Acknowledgments

Thank you, Tanya, for your keen eye and positive words as we worked through the edits. It was a wonderful experience working with you. And thank you to the team at Orca for your hard work and efforts to get our stories into the hands of all readers. A special thank-you to my mom and dad for their constant encouragement.

Cristy Watson is the author of several books for young people, including *Benched* and *Living Rough* in the Orca Currents series. She is also an elementary and middle-school teacher. Cristy lives in Surrey, British Columbia. For more information, visit cristywatsonauthor.wordpress.com.

Cristy
Watson

On Cue

Orca currents

9781459811058 PB

Randi wants to be an actress and is excited
about practicing her craft in drama class. So she
is devastated to learn the program has been cut.
When her friends put together a successful proposal
to have drama class taught as an extracurricular
activity, Randi is thrilled. Until the reality sinks in.
Extracurriculars are scheduled after school, and
after school Randi is expected to take care of her
special-needs brother. Can Randi find a way to
make it all work out?